KU-481-977

The CAN CARAVAN

Richard O'Neill

illustrated by Cindy Kang

Janie was always drawing. She had a great imagination and turned everyday objects into wonderful creations. Her favourite things to sketch were caravans.

She imagined the trailer
she wanted to live in when
she was older and often made
models of her drawings.
Grandad liked helping with
the painting.

Janie was proud of her designs and
loved showing her work to Mrs Tolen,
her grandad's oldest friend.

"You're a chavvie after my own heart, Janie," said Mrs Tolen. "This is a photo of me back when I was training as an engineer. Look at my old lathe!"

"I think Dad had one of those in his workshop," remembered Janie.

"If he was still around I could have borrowed it to fix up this old caravan," said Mrs Tolen, smiling sadly.

At school, Janie's teacher announced that he'd organised a trip to a can recycling plant.

"Does anyone know the history of recycling?" Mr Green asked.

Janie's hand shot up. "Travellers have been recycling for centuries. My grandad told me that his mum collected aluminium pans during the war. The factories needed the metal to make planes."

Janie couldn't wait to tell Mrs Tolen, but her caravan was empty. Mum was outside tending to her plants.

"Have you seen Mrs Tolen?" asked Janie. "I can't find her."

"She's broken her hip and had to go to hospital," said Mum. "Don't worry, though, she'll be okay."

A couple of days later, Janie visited the hospital and took in some official-looking letters.

“Now, what’s all this about?” Mrs Tolen wondered.
“Oh, it’s environmental health. They say my caravan’s not safe. And this one’s from social care. They need to do an assessment so they can find me somewhere else to live.”

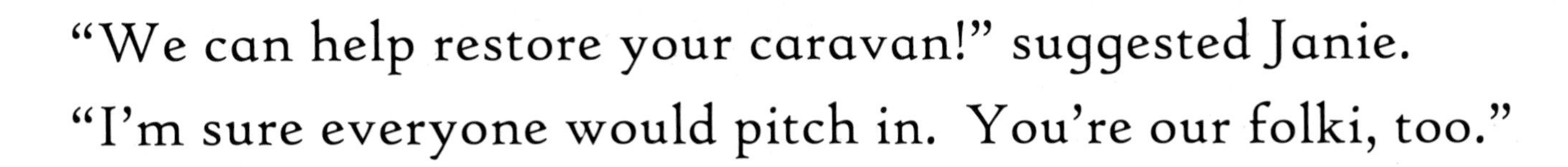

"We can help restore your caravan!" suggested Janie.
"I'm sure everyone would pitch in. You're our folki, too."

"Oh, you're a komli chavvie, but it's too much to ask. I'm an old woman, I'll be fine, they'll find me somewhere."

"But we have to help – you love living on the site!" encouraged Janie.

"Now, Janie," insisted Mrs Tolen, "you must promise on your honour that you won't spend your mum's hard-earned money on my old caravan."

Janie couldn't stop thinking about Mrs Tolen, but the school visit to the can recycling plant distracted her. She couldn't believe the size of the machines.

"This is where the bales come in from the materials recycling facility," explained their guide. "They go up this conveyor belt to be shredded, and then next door where they're melted and cast into huge ingots."

“How many cans does it take to make an ingot?” asked Janie.

“It takes one-and-a-half million cans to make an ingot 10 metres long,” replied an engineer.

The whole class looked shocked. None of them could imagine that many cans!

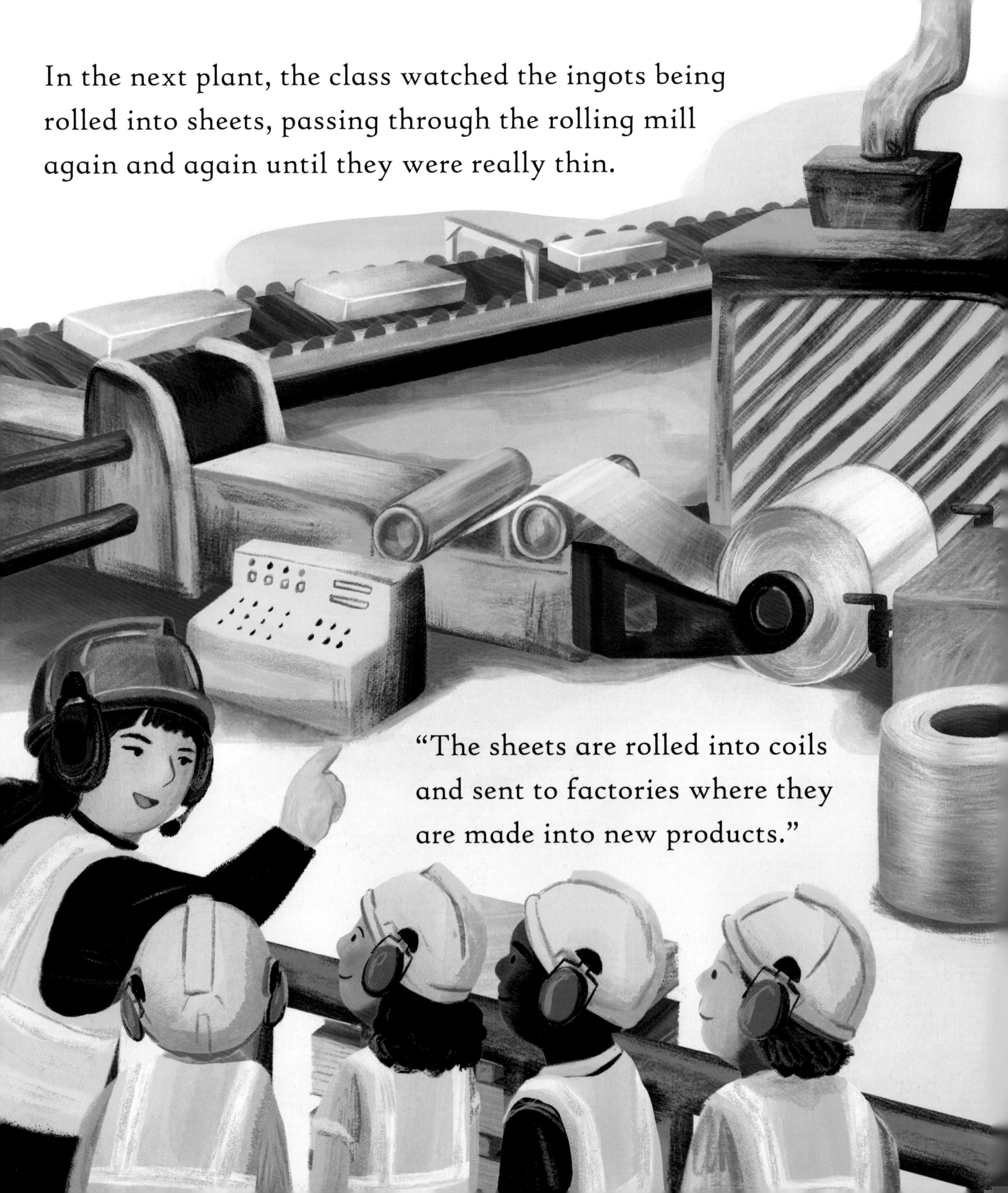

In the next plant, the class watched the ingots being rolled into sheets, passing through the rolling mill again and again until they were really thin.

"The sheets are rolled into coils and sent to factories where they are made into new products."

In the visitors room, the children watched a video of what happens in a can factory. As they watched the aluminium sheets being stamped out and stretched into cup shapes, Janie thought how similar the shape was to an old vardo.

When the engineer mentioned that the sheets were also used to make rockets, an idea popped into her head.

“That’s it!” she almost yelled as she did a quick sketch.

Janie rushed home after school,
bursting with excitement.

"I've got it!" she shouted,
charging through the door.
"We can restore Mrs Tolen's caravan
with recycled aluminium sheets!"

"Great idea," said Mum.
"But you promised Mrs Tolen
we wouldn't spend any money
on her caravan."

"We won't have to," explained Janie.
"We can collect cans to raise money."

"You've got the rag-and-bone trade
in your blood," smiled Grandad.

The next day,
Janie shared her
plans with her class.

"My husband Danny is a welder.
I'm sure he'll help," said Mr Green.

"My dad's an electrician," added Navdeep.

More and more of Janie's
classmates offered their support.

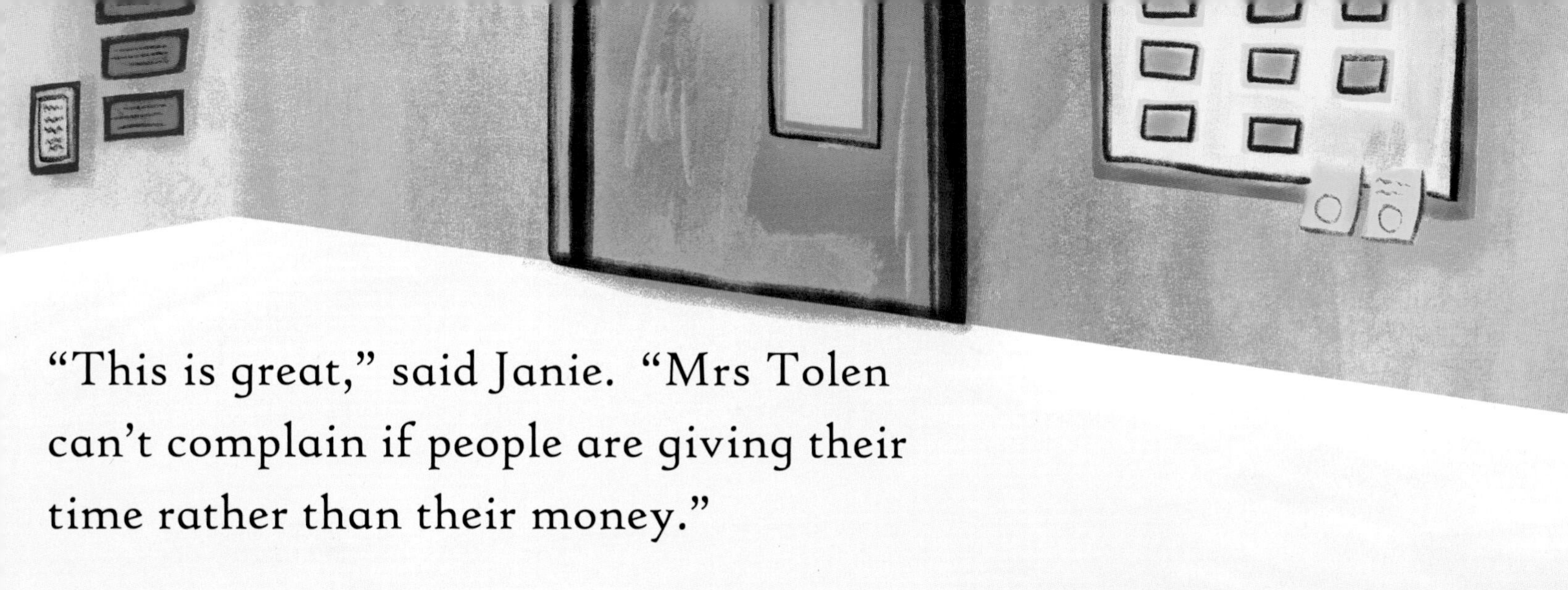

"This is great," said Janie. "Mrs Tolen can't complain if people are giving their time rather than their money."

Together they drew up a list of all the equipment and expertise they would need.

"We'll still need to collect a huge stack of cans, though..." Janie started to feel a little overwhelmed by the size of the project.

"Maybe the recycling plant can help," suggested Imani.

The manager of the rolling mill offered to supply two-thirds of the sheets, but they still needed to collect a lot of cans to cover the rest. Janie needed to get as many people on board as possible.

She made posters and stuck them up all over town.

She spoke in assembly to explain there would be separate bins at school to collect the cans.

She even got her mum's
permission to make
a video to put online.

Soon after that, the local paper got
in touch and word spread even further.

It wasn't long until they had enough
cans and plenty of offers to help!

A couple of weeks later, a truck drove onto the site with the precious aluminium sheets.

Janie's team of helpers got to work immediately. The caravan had already been gutted. Now it was time to rebuild it.

Janie felt a bit daunted being in charge of all the helpers, but she summoned up all her courage.

"Team one, can you make repairs to the frame? Team two, can you start on the wallboards?"

Meanwhile, Mrs Tolen had moved into a care home to have physiotherapy and fully recover. When Janie and Grandad visited, she seemed resigned to living in a house.

"I'm sure they'll find me somewhere nearby. I'll ask when the social worker comes to assess my needs this afternoon."

This gave Janie an idea.

After saying goodbye, Janie and Grandad waited in the car park. They asked everyone arriving if they were the social worker. When she finally found the right person, she explained the plan.

“Well, it’s unusual,” he said, “but if the new caravan meets all the requirements, I don’t see why not. It would have to be checked, but I can do that.”

“Please don’t tell Mrs Tolen,” begged Janie. “We really want it to be a surprise.”

Once the frame was repaired, Navdeep's dad got to work on the electrics. Solar panels were also being fitted to save energy. Mum's friend Callie was making the kitchen from recycled wood.

When the social worker turned up for the inspection, he had some reservations.

"This looks great,
but you'll need a ramp.
The council may be able
to fund one, but it's not
guaranteed," he added.
"And it could take a while."

Janie was trying to figure out what to do, when Danny arrived carrying an aluminium ramp.

"I thought you might need this," he said. "Your grandad is going to help me fit it."

Janie was lost for words.

A week later the caravan was finally finished.

"It's kushti!" said Grandad, as he opened and closed every door and cupboard.

"Do you think Mrs Tolen will like it?" Janie asked.

"Like it? She's going to love it!
I wish your dad was here to see it."

Just then they heard her mum's van
pull up and Janie rushed outside.

“Janie!” Mrs Tolen called. Then she stopped in her tracks. “Whose trailer is that? Have you replaced me already?”

“It’s yours!” Janie smiled. “And we didn’t spend a bar. Everyone helped. Even the recycling plant. It’s made from recycled cans.”

"I can't believe it," Mrs Tolen said,
ready to give Janie a big hug.
"A Can Caravan!"

"The world's first!" Janie grinned.

13. Finished drink cans

ALUMINIUM RECYCLING

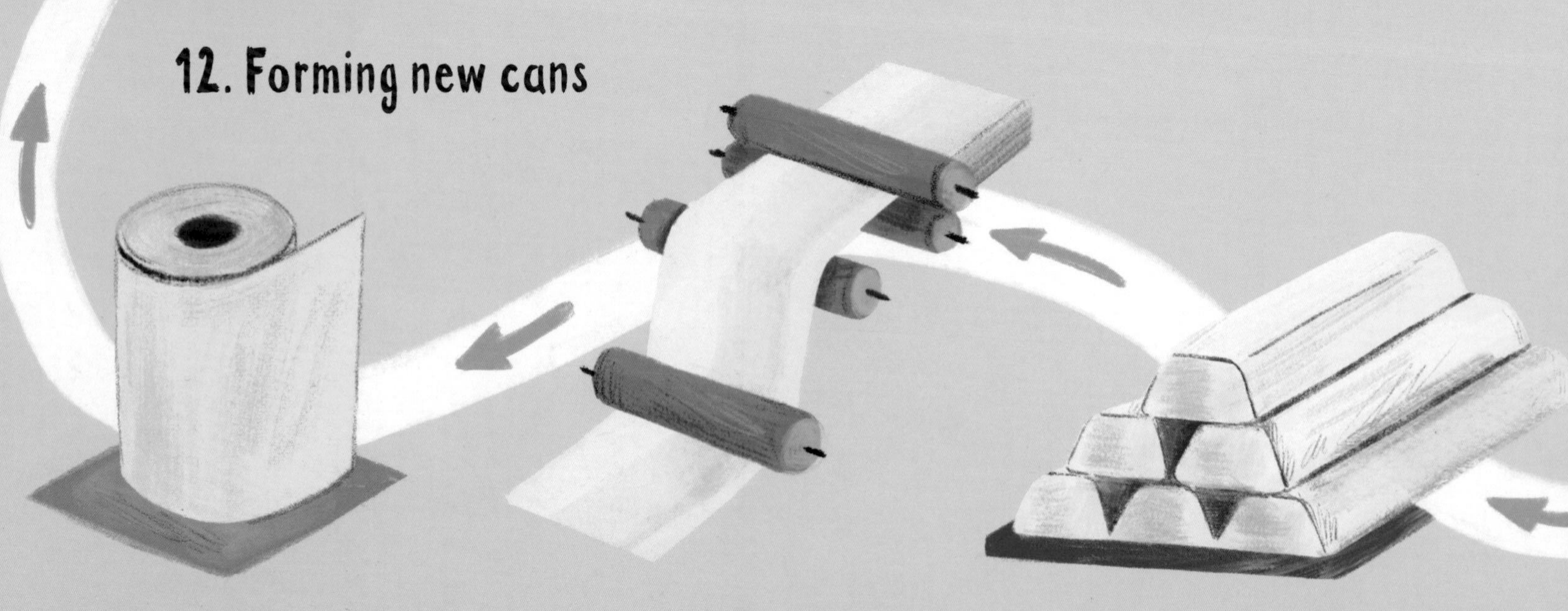

11. Winding into rolls

10. Flattening ingots into sheets